KO'd by LOVE

KATIE O'CONNOR

KO'd by LOVE

Katie O'Connor

Dedication

This one's for Rexx Rally.
Thanks for sharing your boot story with me.
I was more than happy to steal it.

About This Book

About this book
Will helping a stranger refill their Christmas spirit and heal their broken hearts?

Her fiancé dumped and fired Delia Becker last year at Christmas. She's been scrambling ever since to make ends meet. This year, her roommate is having a massive holiday celebration with events every evening for a week. There's no way she wants to be part of that nonsense. In a desperate attempt to run away from life and the holidays, she escapes to her brother's duplex in the ridiculously small town of Crackleberry Ridge. All she wants is time to heal and realign her life.

Nolan Taylor is an MMA fighter on the mend from career-ending injuries sustained in a skiing accident. He's got no degree to fall back on, no prospects for a job, and no hope for the future. Hiding from the press, he runs home to lick his wounds and rethink his plans. Luckily, his newly retired parents have left on a month-long holiday cruise of the Mediterranean and he's got their tiny duplex all to himself.

Both Delia and Nolan want to be left alone. They want nothing to do with Christmas, people, or winter. When a family in need comes their way, they learn a lesson about love and selfishness as they find their hearts.

Chapter One

DECEMBER 1ST

At long last, close to midnight, silence reigned. The Christmas carolers were gone. Nolan couldn't fathom how it took them so long to pass his place. Over an hour from the moment he first heard them until they passed out of hearing. One long, interminable hour. He'd forgotten just how early Crackleberry Ridge began celebrating the holidays.

Judging by the cheerful goodbyes and slamming car doors, the birthday party in the next duplex was finally over as well. It wasn't so much that he disliked Christmas or parties; it was more his inability to concentrate.

He stared out the kitchen window at the snowflakes drifting and swirling in his parent's backyard. *Unbelievable,* he mused, *thirty-four and homeless at Christmas.*

"Bah humbug."

Francine, his mother's grumpy cat, a Seal Point Siamese, hissed her agreement.

Decaf coffee in hand, he fired up his ancient laptop. He'd wallowed long enough. It was time to find a job. But what job was there for a washed-up MMA fighter? He wasn't smart. That's why he'd gotten into fighting. He was fast with his fists and feet and could take on any man twice his size.

He'd been scouted in an Edmonton bar after he took offense at a burly bloke harassing the waitresses and told him to stop. One thing led to another, and their verbal sparring turned to fisticuffs. He didn't hurt the man, he just knocked him to the floor and stood over him until the police arrived.

As luck would have it, the cops let Nolan go without charges, and moments later, Dana White himself was pulling up a chair at his table. The rest was history. For eight years he'd fought match after match. Though he never reached the top spot, he put in a respectable showing in every fight. With a new trainer on his side, he was certain to take the light heavyweight title next summer.

Too bad he'd taken that bit of luck and thrown it away.

He'd been an idiot. What in the world had possessed him to go skiing? He'd never skied in his life. Maybe, now that his injuries were virtually healed, he could go back to school or get a job training new mixed martial arts fighters. The game had changed so much lately, and Lord knew he'd never fight again. Not without risking another fractured shoulder. Until then, he needed to find a temporary position.

Anything to earn enough money to live on. He wasn't going to live at home forever. The past six months of rehab had been enough.

Sighing, he pulled up the first job site and began his twice-daily search.

Something thumped and broke his concentration. "Francine, what are you doing?" he shouted at the cat who had wandered from the room. "Crazy critter." He adored the grumpy beast, but not her penchant for knocking things off the table.

Another thump.

He got up and went searching for whatever she was abusing, only to find her sound asleep under the Christmas tree in her padded, red plaid bed.

"Weird." He returned to the dining room table and his computer.

A loud crash came from next door. Likely the living room, as the two halves of the duplex were mirror images.

"Shoot! Someone's in the neighbor's house." They were on vacation. He pulled out his phone and called 9-1-1.

"Hello, there's someone in my neighbor's house, and he's away on vacation. He didn't mention anything about visitors. I think someone should check." He peered out the kitchen window at the light dancing on the snow in the next yard. "There are lights on and I can see a single shadow."

Minutes later, an RCMP cruiser pulled up out front. He'd expected lights and sirens, but the single officer came in on stealth mode. Curious.

Staying hidden behind the curtains, he hoped for a front-row seat on whatever unfolded.

The officer knocked on the neighbor's door. "RCMP."

Nolan rubbed his hands together in anticipation. He was used to city life. Nothing happened in Crackleberry Ridge. Ever. He could use some excitement that didn't revolve around the holidays.

Someone mumbled. He crept to the front door and eased it open to listen. A soft feminine voice spoke to the officer. She spoke so quietly he didn't catch more than an occasional word, despite straining for all he was worth.

Delia dropped the kettle. Heaven help her, she was so exhausted she could hardly hold the thing up and it was empty. The usual five-hour drive to her brother's house had taken her eight. Traffic was crazy, and the roads were terrible. Fifty miles ago, the snow started falling in thick sheets, just as the wind picked up and threatened to blow her compact car off the road.

It was late. She was tired. And now, someone was pounding on the door of her brother's half of the duplex. Whoever it was, they better not wake the neighbors. The Taylors were in their sixties and didn't need that type of nonsense. Her brother Kyle would kill her if she annoyed them.

She rushed to the front door and peered through the peephole.

"RCMP. Open the door."

A big burly man in uniform stood on her front steps. *What did he want?* She peered past him at the cruiser at the curb. Seemed legit. She slid the chain home and eased the door open.

"Hi."

"Ma'am. I've got a report of a break-in. Can I come in?"

"Can I see some ID?" *As if she'd know real from fake.*

He handed her a badge. She studied it and opened the door. "Come in. What can I do for you, officer?"

"Is this your home?" He stepped inside without closing the door.

Snow swirled inside on a frigid breeze. She wrapped her zip-front hoodie tighter around herself and tucked her hands under her arms.

"No, sir. It is my brother's. He's in Maui now and then in Egypt until February. I'm house-sitting." Not quite a lie, even if it wasn't the absolute truth. She was hiding from her dumpster fire of a life, not house-sitting, but he didn't need to know that.

"I'm going to need some ID and a way to contact the homeowner."

Her knees wobbled. "Oh. Okay. Just let me find my purse." She spun around, her heart pounding. What if he couldn't contact Kyle? Would they arrest her? She tripped over the throw carpet as she raced toward her purse on the dining room table. Her elbow cracked painfully on the coffee table and her leg landed on a rock-solid dog bone. "Crap."

"Do you need help?"

"No, I'm good." Was he laughing at her? Heat flooded her face as she righted herself and dug through her purse. "I know my wallet is here. I used it in Canmore to buy gas."

The officer made a noncommittal noise.

She dug again. Then dumped the contents on the scarred pine table. "Oh, my gosh. It isn't here." She turned to stare at the officer and whirled back to the mess on the table. "Shoot. Oh, hockey pucks. It must be in my car." *I hope it's in my car. I'll be double-hooped if I can't find it. He'll arrest me for sure.*

She raced past him, out the door, to her car. The snow immediately soaked her feet. She rushed back in, grabbed her keys off the table beside the door, and raced back out, shoeless.

She dove in and started digging through the trash on her seat and floor and jerked up triumphantly, wallet in hand, slamming her head on the rearview mirror. "Ouch."

"Are you okay?"

She screamed and jumped, banging her head again. "Ouch." She mumbled a few choice words under her breath. "Don't do that," she snapped. "Oh, no." She slapped a hand over her mouth and mumbled an apology to the officer. "Sorry. I'm kind of freaked out."

"Relax, ma'am. I'm just here to ensure nothing untoward is happening." He took three steps back but still kept one hand on her car door. Did he think she was going to drive off?

"Um. My feet are freezing." She waggled her wet socks at him. "Can we go back inside?"

She managed to produce her driver's license but failed to reach her brother on the phone. "Um. Er." she stammered and stretched for something to prevent her being arrested. The officer's expression vacillated between annoyed and amused. "I know." She snapped her fingers.

"Come inside. Look at the pictures." She jabbed a finger at a corner shelf laden with family pictures.

Stomping off his boots and wiping them carefully, he strode to the shelf. He looked at the pictures, then at her, and back at the pictures. He picked up a birthday card off the coffee table. "This is you; I assume?" He gestured with the rude card she'd given her brother for his birthday.

"Ya." She sighed. "That's me. We're twins." She didn't know how else to explain it. They had a fabulous love-torture bond.

"Look," he said at long last. "I'm going to take down all your information. I can see that you are, in some fashion, connected to the person who lives here. The pictures are evidence of that. But I will be following up with your brother by phone. Do not leave town without consulting me." He handed her a card, copied her information off her license took five minutes' worth of notes, and left after saying, "I'm just going to reassure the caller that everything is on the up and up. You might want to keep the noise down, just to avoid annoying him again." He tipped his hat and walked out the front door.

She peeked out the open door and watched as he walked up to the Taylor's front door. She glared past him at the attractive young man who opened the door. Did the Taylor's move? Kyle didn't mention it. If they hadn't moved, why was that guy, that drool-worthy guy in their house? She'd be making some phone calls of her own to find out who he was and why he was there. She didn't trust him one bit. He was too tall, too handsome, and too broad-shouldered for her liking. Something dormant winked back to life inside her.

Chapter Two

Nolan lay in bed, staring at the ceiling. He really should get up and restart his job hunt, but his shoulder ached, and his heart just wasn't into it. After the kerfuffle next door, the rest of the night passed blissfully in total quiet. The woman next door must be legit. At least, that's what the officer had told him. When his folks checked in, he'd find out if the guy next door even had a sister.

He sat on the edge of his childhood bed, rotated his shoulders, and began his physio stretches. Three times a day, whether he wanted to do them or not. Everything by the book. He might not fight again, but he wanted to avoid reinjury in the future. Rehab was a pain in the butt.

The doorbell rang. He glanced at the bedside clock. "Seven-fifty-two? Who's even up at this hour?" Wincing with morning stiffness, he stepped into his ratty workout sweats and headed for the door.

"Ya?" he snapped as he flung the door open.

"Good morning!" The perkiest blonde, blue-eyed nymph he'd ever seen stood on his steps in winter boots and a navy sweater with snowflakes all over it. She looked like a pixie, or heaven forbid, a Christmas elf. Her hair brushed her shoulders, and her eyes were bright with a smile.

She thrust a cloth-covered basket at him.

He grunted as it made contact with his abs. He grabbed the handle and eased it away from his stomach.

"I made muffins. I couldn't sleep, so I got up and baked. It's the least I could do since my arrival disturbed you last night. "I'm Delia Becker. Kyle's sister. He's on vacation and I'm house-sitting." She jabbed a hand toward him. "Nice to meet you."

He stared at her hand, the basket, and then the snow drifting down. The flakes melted on her hair and sparkled like diamonds in the porch light. It was still dark outside. Who got up this early and baked? Lunatics, that's who. She better not be one of those holiday junkies out to make everyone fall in love with Christmas.

"Thanks?" He stepped back to go inside. She didn't release the basket. He tugged at it. "I'll get the basket back to you."

She dropped her hands, and a small frown appeared between her perfectly arched brows. *Was he supposed to invite her in? It wasn't even eight.*

She reached out and lifted the cloth. "These are blueberry, and these are apple crumble. I hope you like them. She dropped the cloth back in place.

"Thanks. I'll let you know how they are." Her pert lips turned down. He hadn't meant to be mean, but he was not a morning person by any stretch of the imagination. He hadn't taken his pain meds, and she was entirely too perky for dawn.

"Fine. Nice meeting you. Whoever you are." Sarcasm dripped from her words. She stormed down the steps.

Guilt stabbed him in the chest. Perhaps he could have been nicer.

The man was an ingrate.

"I'm Nolan. Thank you." His words were muffled by the falling snow.

She ignored him. What kind of man called the cops on his neighbor for a bit of noise, and then refused to say thanks for an apology gift? She'd spent over an hour on those stupid muffins and had given him all of them.

Her stomach growled. She glared down at it. "Shut up."

Their front doors were only twenty feet apart but had separate sidewalks. She stomped down his and up hers, narrowly avoiding falling on her face when she slipped on the fresh snow. Dang, now she'd have to shovel. She'd forgotten that part of small-town living. In the city, she always woke to shoveled sidewalks outside her apartment.

Her phone was ringing when she got back inside. She raced to the kitchen.

"Hi, Kyle," she answered, half breathless. "Why didn't you answer last night? I needed you."

"Ya, I got that when the police woke me up with a call. What happened?"

"What happened?" She winced when her voice rose to near Karen status. "Your neighbor, who isn't the Taylors, by the way, called the police on me and said I was a robber. I was nearly arrested. All because I wanted a few days away from Christmas. And why did you decorate before you left? Am I supposed to put this junk away?"

"Chill, Delia. That guy is their son. He's house-sitting. Give him a break. He's recovering from an accident that ended his fighting career."

"You can have a career in fighting? Jeez."

"Mixed martial arts. The UFC? Cage fighting? It's a real skill test, and he was on track to become one of the best."

"Huh. Well, I'm sorry he was hurt, but he's grumpy. He didn't even seem pleased that I gave him muffins."

"Tell me you didn't go over there this early." He groaned. "Delia. It's Sunday. Nobody is up this early. I never understood your drive to be up and busy by five."

"Ha. I slept in until sixty-thirty." Her brother, Kyle, was a sloth. He took the afternoon medic shifts so he could sleep in every day. Who did that?

"Still too early for normal humans on the weekend. Besides, you're on vacation. Rest. Relax. Enjoy Christmas."

"Bah, humbug. I came here to avoid Christmas. Although looking around your place, it looks like Christmas exploded."

"Don't be a Scrooge. Cindy and I love the holidays. If the decorations offend you, you could go home. I'd hire my usual house sitter instead of letting you live rent-free for two months and paying her fee to you."

He was teasing, but it still hurt. She didn't ask to be fired and dumped all at once by the same man. Her ex-fiancé was a total dweeb. Looking back, she didn't know how or why she fell for him in the first place..

"Look, sis. Why don't you get a part-time job or something? Everyone's looking for holiday help. Or write that novel you've been procrastinating on. Isn't it due soon? Just leave the neighbors alone."

"Fine. I'll leave him alone, and I'm taking down these decorations. I have zero Christmas spirit, and this makes me want to gag."

"Oh, Dee. Forget the jerk who dumped you at Christmas. There's joy and beauty all around you. Remember, Mom always told us to find the good. Every cloud has a silver lining. You're destined for great things, I know it. I believe in you. Believe in yourself."

She wiped away a tear. Kyle always had her back, but he really didn't understand her. She wanted to have a successful career, be married, and have kids. Thirty-two was pushing the limits. Sure, women older than her had kids, but she wanted them now.

"Thanks, bro. I'll try and cheer up." And she'd darn well avoid Mr. Grumpy next door. Nathan or Nolan, or whatever his name was, wasn't getting any more baked treats. Not one. "Love you, Kyle. Say hi to Cindy and enjoy your vacation."

"The vacation is great, and I can't wait to start my research in Egypt. Cindy's excited too."

Jealously rocked her. There he was, living her dream. Engaged, traveling, doing what he loved, seeing the world, with a solid plan for the family they'd have. She was so happy for him. Sadly, she was jealous as well. "Catch you later. Bye."

She hung up and set the phone down. This was not how she planned to start her vacation. It was supposed to be a turning point in her life. She'd find a new job, maybe not in Edmonton where she was from. Maybe it was time to widen her horizons and consider moving somewhere else. Maybe she could get a job overseas.

Weirdly buoyed and depressed, she put on a fresh pot of coffee and went to have a shower.

Chapter Three

T hough his shoulder ached like the dickens this morning, Nolan grabbed the shovel from the garage and headed outside. The snow was still falling, but he wanted to clear it before it piled too high. Even now, two inches was a lot to move. He'd have to go slow or risk reinjuring himself.

Snuggled into his warmest red plaid flannel jacket, or bush jacket as his family called it, he cleared the steps and hummed along to the music throbbing through the walls of the house next door. It wasn't all that loud. He hadn't even heard it when he was inside. But out here, a hint of music slipped through the window Miss Muffins had cracked open. At least she had good taste in music.

He shoveled and hummed. Abruptly, the music stopped.

Ten seconds later, her voice broke through the frigid morning air. "What are you doing?"

He lifted his head and straightened his back. *Man, I ache already.* "Shoveling?"

"Ya, I can see that. That's my sidewalk."

"Yup." He banked a grin at the fire in her eyes and her crossed arms. She shivered in the cold on her front step.

"Why are you clearing my walk?" She rubbed her hands up and down her arms.

"I don't know. I just started mine and kept going. It feels good to work." He paused. "Consider it payment for the delicious muffins. They're very good."

"You're welcome." She pivoted and stomped back toward the house. "Thanks for shoveling. Come inside when you're done. I've just made coffee."

She stormed up the steps, her backside bouncing nicely in her snug jeans. She had an adorable shape. Curvy and fit, if he was any judge of the female form. He turned his eyes away. He wasn't the type to ogle a woman. But somehow, between her generosity with the muffins, and her prickly manners, she fascinated him. He smiled for the first time in weeks. Maybe having a youthful neighbor wasn't going to be all bad.

He shoveled both front walks and the stretch alongside the road. Setting the shovel on his step, he decided he'd tackle the back later. Or tomorrow. Right now, he had an attractive neighbor offering coffee. Being a good son, he'd stop in and keep up positive neighborly relations.

He knocked lightly and after a moment; the door swung inward.

"Thanks," she said at the exact moment he started saying, "Thanks for the invitation."

She giggled. "Great minds think alike." She stepped back and waved him inside. "Come in, N-" Her cheeks pinkened. "Sorry. I forgot your name."

"Nolan Tayler." He removed his mittens and offered his hand.

"Delia Becker. My friends call me Dee."

Her hand was soft and warm against his icy fingers.

"Oh, you're freezing. Get in here." She tugged him into the warm house. "Get that jacket off. You'll warm up quicker. I made cookies."

"Cookies and muffins in one day? Are you a baker by trade?"

"Stress baker. I am, or rather I was, in advertising and graphic design. I'm currently looking for work."

"You and me both."

"Ya, I read about your accident. Sorry to hear what happened to you."

She read about his accident. Who googled strangers? And if she did, why didn't she remember his name? Curious.

"Life's tough. I'll find a new career." Saying the words aloud sparked a tiny bit of optimism, which winked in his mind as he followed her into the kitchen after hanging his jacket on a classic wooden coat rack. The entire main floor was littered with holiday décor. Pillows, rows of Santas, and snowmen. A huge live tree nestled in the bay living room window, though the lights were off. It made his undecorated place seem cold and lifeless. He half wished his parents had decorated before they left.

"Good for you." Her words rang with encouragement. "Just so you know, this is my brother's place. I'm house-sitting. Kyle, my brother, told me you were staying with your folks while you rehab. Where are you from?"

"Didn't you find that on your snoopy search?" he teased and was rewarded with a guilty pink in her cheeks.

"Actually no. I watched some news clips and some fights. That stuff is brutal. I don't know how you could do that for a living." She shuddered. "Coffee?"

"Sure."

She poured coffee into two thick, holiday-painted, ceramic mugs and set them on the table beside a trio of snowmen, the cream and sugar, and a heaping plate of peanut butter cookies and gingersnaps. "Help yourself and tell me about fighting."

"Honestly? I was a brat growing up, and I liked to pick fights. I won most of them until I picked a fight with the wrong guy, and he beat the crap out of me." He shrugged. "I decided that wouldn't happen again, so I took up karate when I was fourteen."

She leaned forward and gave him her full attention.

"Eventually, by the time I was eighteen, I learned there was honor in winning an even fight, and none in bullying. When I got my black belt, I added Ju-Jitsu. Then Muay Thai. I trained seven days a week. I had a coach steer me toward The Octagon. It was six years before Dana White scouted me and got a replacement slot in the UFC. Thank heaven I won."

"And you kept on winning. You climbed the ranks quickly. It's so terrible that you crashed when you were skiing."

"Bad luck for me. In hindsight, I should have taken a lesson or two before I attempted the harder ski runs. But I was cocky and now I'm paying for it." It was hard to admit that he'd been stupid. It seemed like his entire life was the result of stupid decisions.

"So, what now?" She sipped her coffee without taking her eyes off him.

"Find a job that pays the bills. I'm nearly healed, though hard labor is out of the question for a while."

"Coaching? Can you teach karate? Or one of those other things?"

"That may be an eventual possibility." He sipped his coffee. "Is that cinnamon in the coffee?" It was weird, but not bad. He sipped again. "Different."

"Good different, or bad different?"

"I'm not certain. I wasn't expecting it. It's okay. Enough about me. What about you?"

"No real story. I'm looking for a new job. Expanding my search area. No leads yet. I've been waiting tables until something else comes along. I'm on sabbatical." She rolled her eyes. "That's the polite way of saying that I'm running away from my roommate's crazy holiday plans—lots of big parties. My ex will be there. If I were there too, it would get ugly. You know the drill."

"Unfortunately, I do." He raised his mug. "Here's to two unemployed friends, hiding out, trying to find work, and getting their ducks in a row."

They clinked mugs.

"Ducks? Man, I've got squirrels and they're not in a row. They're at a rave." She laughed.

They touched mugs again. Comfortable silence fell.

"How are you filling your time?" he asked. "Aside from baking." He selected a peanut butter cookie and bit into it. "Oh, man. These are the best. You could open a bakery."

Delia considered the idea. "No. I don't think so. Baking is fun but I wouldn't want to do it full time. It's a hobby thing."

"I noticed that your tree is unlit, but the place is decorated to the nines." He looked around. Greenery hung on all the door frames. Little knickknacks and ornaments littered most surfaces. Even their mugs and the cookie plate were Christmas themed. As were the salt and pepper shakers on the back of the stove.

"Not my place, remember? It's my brother's. He said he wasn't going to decorate, but apparently, his girlfriend changed his mind. I'm going to start taking it down today." She used to love Christmas.

"Why bother? It's already up."

"I'm not feeling the least bit Christmassy." She shrugged. "I'm boycotting this year's holidays. I just want to be alone to discover who I am." *And forget about what my jerk of an ex did to me.* After five years, she was certain she'd get a ring at Christmas. Instead, she got her walking papers. From his life, and his company. "Last year was the worst Christmas ever." She tried not to sigh, or sound like she was whining, but deep inside, she knew she failed at both.

"Give it a day or two," he advised. "You might change your mind. That is a lovely tree. Douglas fir, I think."

"I'll think about thinking about it. That's all I've got."

His deep laughter startled her. "Delia, that's the funniest thing I've heard all week." He finished his coffee and stood. "But I should go. I'll be around if you need anything."

"Thanks, and the next shoveling is on me."

Chapter Four

Delia made so many batches of cookies that she was out of butter, margarine, sprinkles, and vanilla. Since the snowy, blustery weather warmed up to just below freezing, it was the perfect day for a walk. She met friendly face after friendly face on her walk to the grocery store. Everyone greeted her with a warm hello, or a Merry Christmas. The camaraderie was sweet and by the time she'd walked six blocks through downtown Crackleberry Ridge; she was feeling like a local. It was about as far from the big city as it got, and she loved it. Even the abundance of Christmas decorations and carols ringing through the air didn't burst her bubble.

She paused outside the pet store window to admire a golden retriever puppy wearing a big red bow. The puppy wiggled excitedly when she tapped on the glass. Pets were another item on her bucket list, not that she could have one in her pet-free building. Tenants couldn't even have fish. When she'd been fresh out of college and brimming with success at her new job, pets didn't seem like a big deal or a necessity. Now, she was rethinking that decision. Too bad Kyle had put his dog in a kennel while he was gone. She would have enjoyed the company.

With a hint of resurging melancholy hanging over her shoulders, she trudged the last half a block, crossed the grocery store's slushy parking lot, and entered through the automatic doors into blessed heat. Stamping her feet to clear off the slush, she peered into the depths of Markam's Grocery. It was bigger than she expected. The lighting was bright, the aisles long. The meat department was huge with signs advertising beef, pork, chicken, and bison. She grabbed a cart which, lo-and-behold, didn't require a Loonie. She tucked the Canadian dollar coin back in her pocket and headed in, shucking her toque and mitts as she went.

She wandered slowly, warming up as she shopped. She was paused before the meat counter when a familiar voice greeted her.

"Fancy meeting you here." Nolan stopped his cart beside hers.

"It is the only grocery store in town." She kept her tone light. The other day, in her kitchen, they'd passed from enemies at first glance to something that felt like the beginning of a friendship. She didn't want to disturb that fragile accord. And, if she were to admit it to herself, his initial rudeness when she gave him muffins still annoyed her.

"Yup. The only one. Unless you count Moxie's Madness, the convenience store attached to the Gas Barn, which I don't. What are you buying?"

"Food?" How were any of her purchases his business?

He peered into her cart. "Not that I can see. Looks pretty empty." He looked her up and down. "Going on a diet?"

"You did not just say that." She glared, slammed a beef roast into her cart, and pushed away.

"Delia, wait. I didn't mean it like that. I was teasing. Your cart is empty." He chased along after her, abandoning his cart behind him.

"I just arrived." *Ooh, the man was a jerk.* Kyle said he was a great guy, just in a tough spot. Well, no wonder he was having trouble. He was a Grade A Wiener. "There's a good chance I'll fill my cart as I go." She turned her back on him.

"Look. I really am sorry. You're right."

The background music morphed from *Frosty* to *Forgive and Forget at Christmas*. Nolan shot past her and turned to face her. He made a grand gesture toward the ceiling speakers. "See, even the music is on my side. Come on. Please. Give me a chance. They rarely let me out in public."

The outrageous comment made her laugh. "You know you're crazy, right?"

He burst into song, "*Crazy...*"

She held up a hand. "Stop right now. Or I'll reconsider my possible forgiveness. Your voice is terrible."

He threw a hand over his eyes and mimed wiping away tears. "You wound me, fair lady."

"If I forgive you, will you drop the theatrics? Please." She edged her cart backward, toward the meat section, and put the roast back where she found it. With a pound of ground beef and a small package of pork chops, she started forward again. He was still there, watching her.

"Am I forgiven?" His voice was pure and serious, and his expression cautious.

"Fine. I forgive you. Now, if you'd scoot your cart out of the way, there's a block of Gouda calling my name."

"Brie is a better cheese," he challenged as he shifted out of the center of the aisle.

"Philistine. Brie is in no way superior to Gouda." They walked up and down the aisles bickering good-naturedly about different food preferences, and which was the ultimate Christmas song.

"I'm telling you, it's *God Rest Ye Merry Gentlemen.*" She crossed her arms over her chest and snorted when he rolled his eyes.

"*Winter Wonderland.* Or *Mary's Boy Child.*"

When they got to the register, the perky teenage cashier said, "This is the first time I ever saw a married couple get two carts. At least with so little in them. You guys new in town?"

They looked at each other and started to laugh. They laughed until tears ran down Delia's face. "Oh, no. We're not a couple. We just met yesterday. I'm staying at my brother's."

"And I'm staying at my folks. I've lived here for six months."

"Oh. Well, you joke fight just like my mom and dad." She shrugged and started ringing through Nolan's small order.

He was waiting for her by the door after she checked out. "Oh, I thought you'd be gone." *Why was he still here?*

"There are no cars in the lot, so I assumed you walked like I did. I thought company would be nice on the way home."

"Well, we're going the same way, so why not?"

"That's the spirit."

She set her reusable bags on the sidewalk, zipped up, and pulled on her mitts and toque. "Aren't you cold?" She stared at his hatless head.

"Not really. I miss the cold. I spent the last few years living and training in Vegas. The snow is refreshing."

"The more I know about you, the weirder you are." She laughed to take the sting out of her words.

"Why thank you." He bowed low and picked up her heaviest bag, the one with the sugar. "I'll carry this one." They walked side by side, past the now dark pet store, the post office, and the pharmacy. "Do you want to get a drink? There's a pub around the corner."

"Okay?" She didn't have any groceries that would be harmed by half an hour in the freezing temperatures, so why not? They turned left and walked past the public library and were there.

The pub was a converted, Victorian style home, complete with a generous covered porch and dormer windows. It was also lit up bright enough to be seen from space. She tried to hide her wince. *So much for avoiding the holiday.*

Nolan paused. "I forgot about the lights. You okay to go in, despite the cheer?"

"I'm not that fragile. I'll survive a bit of holiday cheer for the sake of a cup of cocoa with a shot."

"Is that two separate drinks or just one?"

"That'll be one. Hot chocolate with either Kahlua, Baileys, or peppermint Schnapps. And a huge dollop of whipped cream." She rubbed her tummy through her jacket like she was starving. "Let's do this."

A six-foot tall, motion-activated Santa greeted them in the small entryway with a jolly ho-ho-ho. And unfortunately, things went downhill after that. A live band played holiday tunes. There were lights and streamers everywhere. Servers dressed as elves; the bartender wore a red velvet vest with fur trim and a matching Santa hat. The only thing that didn't scream Christmas was the blue neon sign proclaiming, "Welcome to Joe's."

She banked a sigh. If she didn't know better, she'd think the universe was trying to tell her something. She slid between two tables and headed for the last empty table near the back. She sensed Nolan right behind her.

Their groceries went on two empty chairs as a broad-shouldered elf sidled up to them. "Merry Christmas, folks. What can I getcha?" He shouted to be heard over the musicians.

Nolan waved for her to go first.

"I'll have a hot chocolate with Kahlua and a mountain of whipped cream."

The server grinned. "You betcha. And you, sir?"

"Irish coffee please, with Jameson's. Easy on the topping."

"On it, boss." He hurried away.

She shed her jacket and sat down. The band took a break, and the noise level dropped to near tolerable. "Whew. That's better." She studied the room. "I like this place. It's clean. It's fun."

"It's Christmas central." He sat across from her. "I apologize for that."

"Nolan, it's okay. It's Christmas whether I want it to be or not. I'll survive. You don't have to mince around it like you're walking on eggshells. My distaste is my own and not something you have to worry about."

"Honestly, I'm not super keen on the holidays this year. It's my first Christmas without my folks and my sister. She's gone to Disneyland with her family and Mom and Dad are on a cruise."

"Christmas alone sounds lonely."

"Says the woman staying alone in a strange town."

Their server slid their drinks on the table. "I started a tab for you. You can pay at the bar when you're done."

Nolan slipped him a tip, and the man nodded his thanks and hurried away.

"I am alone in a strange town. Well, I've been here to visit my brother before. I know your folks and a few others. But coming here was my idea. My choice."

"What led to that decision? If you don't mind me asking."

"Desperation." She laughed wryly and rolled her eyes. "My roommate still works for the company that let me go. My ex owns the company. She'll invite him to all her parties and frankly, if I never see him again, it'll be too soon."

Nolan winced. "That sucks for you. Maybe you'll find some peace here. If I stop taking you to all the holiday hot spots."

She fondled the fake pine surrounding the battery-operated candle on their table. "It's not so bad. For a pub, it looks pretty good."

Chapter Five

Nolan did his best to tune out the band when they started playing again. They were too loud for his liking, but Delia was keeping time with her fingers tapping. He and Delia were discussing ordering another round when his mother's friend and neighbor strode up.

"Nolan, don't forget the toy drive on Friday."

"The what now?" he stared at Mrs. Anderson like she'd lost her mind.

"The Santa's Helper toy drive. Your folks help out every year. Your dad rents a van, and we drive around to all the businesses collecting food and toy donations. Unlike the city, we only have one drive that covers everything. There will be clothing and jackets too. It's a bundle of work."

"I imagine it would be." *Was she expecting him to take part in the collection?*

"Good. We'll see you at the Catholic church at four on Friday. Dress warm."

"I'm sorry. Are you asking for help? I don't mind, but-"

"Didn't your mother tell you? She said she would. Oh dear. We've got a replacement for your mom, but without your dad to drive we'll be short. We did get a van, but she assured us you'd pitch in. This is terrible." Her voice wobbled, and she twisted her hands together.

"Ma'am. I'm Delia. Nolan and I will be pleased to pitch in. We're happy to help."

"Oh, you dear girl. Thank you so much. This means a lot to the community. You're helping over a hundred people. You have such a generous heart." She turned her attention back to Nolan. "Son, you hang onto this one. She's a keeper."

"She sure is." He gave her a side-eye. "See you Friday, Mrs. Anderson." He watched her make her unsteady way back across the bar.

"I'm sorry." Delia grabbed his hand. "I shouldn't have volunteered you. But she's much too old to do this alone. I couldn't help myself. If you don't want to help, I'll go alone."

He shrugged. "Apparently my mother already vol-untold me, so it's all good. I'm sure they'll be happy to have us both." He grinned. "We should get out of here before we get rooked into something else."

Friday evening, inside the hardware store, Delia stared at the boot. "Holy moly."

"You've got that right." The red and white wooden cowboy boot was a full five feet tall, and brimming with packages and bags. It was far too heavy to shift or tip over. How were they supposed to get the donations out of that thing? "I wonder who had the bright idea to use this monstrosity for collection. Where do you even get something like this?" He looked like he'd bitten something sour.

"I think it's adorable. This is Alberta. This massive boot perfectly sums up the province. I mean, just look at the wheat." She smiled. Someone had decorated it with a carved prairie and mountain scene, right down to cows, bears, and a beaver.

"If you say so." He looked the boot up and down. "I'll pass you the gifts. You put them in the boxes?"

"Teamwork. I like it." She rubbed her hands together in anticipation. It was kind of fun to gather gifts. This was their fifth and final stop. She was having a blast but was ready to be finished. Sometimes even the fun jobs last too long. Working together, they quickly assembled some boxes and taped the bottoms.

The first bit was easy. Nolan handed her bags of unwrapped gifts, some clothing, a toaster, and some food donations. Each went into a box. "I'm trying to sort a bit as we go. You know, gifts separate from food." She slipped a bingo game into a box beside several decks of cards.

"Great idea. That'll make the next step easier for the other volunteers." He handed her a couple of board games. "Some poor kid is getting Scrabble."

"Lucky kid. I love Scrabble. I adore word games."

"And to think I was starting to like you." He winked and handed over a cuddly doll and a teddy bear. "I guess everyone has questionable qualities."

"Apparently. I mean, look at you. You don't like word games. What type of ill-mannered wretch are you?" She slid three books into a box.

"The best kind." He leaned into the boot. "I can barely reach these. I need a stool or something."

The stool wasn't much help. It was five feet to the bottom of the boot and, by the look of things, the toe had been stuffed as well. "I almost need to be inside to get the rest of these, but I don't dare climb in. I'd wreck something by stepping on it."

They stared at the boot. Then at each other.

"I could..." he trailed off and shook his head.

"You could what?" She had a feeling she wouldn't like what he was about to say.

"I could lift you up and hold your ankles and dip you in, headfirst. You could pass the gifts back up to me. At least until we can see the bottom."

"That's nuts." She tapped her finger on her lips. "There has to be a better way. I mean, they must have done this before." The store was swamped with Christmas shoppers, and they didn't want to disturb the already busy staff. "Do you see another option?" she asked, dreading going headfirst into the boot.

"Honestly, no. But I can hold you. You're pretty small."

She was average, but she decided to take his words as a compliment. She stepped out of her heavy winter boots. "Okay, let's do this. But if you drop me..."

"I won't drop you. I swear. Cross my heart." He made an enormous X over his heart and smiled seriously. "You are completely safe in my hands."

Stepping up to the boot, she tried to peer over the edge. She could barely see into it. She banked her fear. "Lift me so I can bend over the edge." Luckily, the boot's edge was thick and rounded. She could hang there for a moment until he got a good grip on her feet. He boosted her up, and she leaned forward. "Grab my feet."

His hands wormed under the ends of her jeans and grasped her bare ankles above her socks.

"Yikes, your hands are freezing."

"Sorry. Are you ready?"

She grunted her agreement. He lifted her legs, and she inched over the edge. "Further. I can't quite reach." He lifted higher, and she slid over the lip and stretched out to grab a microscope set. "Got one." It was heavier than she expected. "Oof." Gripping it with both hands, she raised it up and over her head, back towards the rim of the boot.

Nolan released one ankle to grab it. She started slipping.

"Don't let me fall," she screamed and crashed, headfirst, into the bottom of the boot. She hit hard, her head bent sideways at an awkward angle, feet in the air, with the corner of the microscope box jabbing into her back. "Nolan!" She screamed. "Get me out of here." She wasn't hurt, but the position was painful.

He groaned. "Gimme a sec. I think I pulled something." He muttered and cussed.

"Are you okay?" She gasped for breath. All her blood was pooling in her head, and she was getting dizzy. She struggled to get her hands under her and push herself to the top again. Finally, with her hands below her crooked head, she pushed upward. The toys under her left hand shifted, and she slipped and wedged herself sideways with something sharp jabbing into her side.

She wiggled again and managed to get herself completely stuck. "Nolan." She groaned. "Get me out of here before I suffocate."

A shadow blocked the light coming in. "You won't suffocate. There's a ton of air in there. The manager is getting help."

She waited and waited. Her already low Christmas spirit ebbed faster than a megastar's popularity after they did something stupid. And this, being upside down in a boot, was stupid on a whole new level.

Minutes passed, feeling like hours. Nolan stood over her, offering encouragement.

"Just grab my legs and yank me out."

"I can't."

"You put me in here, you can get me out."

A bright light flashed, nearly blinding her, despite being face down.

"Are you taking pictures?" Three more flashes. "Get me out!" She gasped for air. The pressure on her chest and in her brain hurt like the dickens.

"I can't, I'm sorry. I overestimated the strength of my bad shoulder and underestimated your weight. I tweaked something trying to hold you one-handed.

She grumbled to herself about the indignity of it all and how she was going to maim him when she got out. A deep voice interrupted her grumbling.

"Hang tight, ma'am. We'll get you right out of there. It'll just be a quick second."

Wait! What! Who was that? The manager? "Okay."

"We're just grabbing two ladders."

"How's that going to help?" She muttered. It was too tight in the boot to turn around, and there was zero room for a ladder.

"Hang tight, Delia," Nolan called as if she could do anything else.

The microscope box lifted off her back, taking its stabby corner with it. "We're going to wrap your ankles to protect them."

Protect them? What were they planning? "Whatever." She didn't care what they did as long as they hurried.

Soft cloth wrapped around each of her ankles.

"We're going to lift now. On three. One, two, three."

Slowly, her back straightened and the pressure against her face and chest eased. Flashes went off. Someone called, "Are you recording this? This is hilarious."

She wiggled, trying to see what was happening.

"Don't move. Let your body relax and you'll be out faster than Santa can pop down the chimney."

Her head finally crested the edge. Two burly firefighters stood on ladders on either side of the boot. Each of them had one of her cloth-wrapped ankles in their hands. Two more firefighters reached out and grasped her by the waist, pulled her over so she hung by the waist over the edge of the boot. This time, her feet were inside.

She gasped for the air she'd been longing for. Even though she was bent over the boot edge at the waist, she greedily sucked in much needed oxygen. Nolan stood to the side, cradling his shoulder with his other hand and looking extremely repentant.

Eventually, with much shifting and struggling, they managed to get her on her feet. "Take a seat, miss. We'll just assess you for damage. You could have hurt something in that fall."

The man turned to Nolan. "And you, sir, we'll check you over next. Why didn't you use the rope ladder?"

"What ladder?" Delia and Nolan answered in unison.

"The boot was designed with a ladder. It clips here," he pointed to two discreet hooks, "and flips inside. You climb in, rung by rung, as you empty it."

"That would have been so much easier," Nolan said. He winced as a medic prodded his shoulder. "Ouch. I'm good. I see my physio tomorrow. She'll check it over. Look after Delia."

A few more flashes went off and a short man with a mustache approached them. "I'm Hank Tallow, editor of the Crackleberry Ridge Tattler. I'd like to get some statements about what happened."

"I'll tell you what happened," Delia snapped. "This jerk thought it would be fun to drop me into the boot." She rubbed her cheeks. "My face is killing me."

"Ya. It's got some nice bruises coming." Tallow snapped another picture.

"I've got nothing to say." She turned away, wincing as her small scrapes pulled.

Nolan, the medics, and the firefighters talked with the reporter for a few minutes as she studiously ignored them all. Eventually, the crowd cleared, and someone produced the rope ladder they should have had to begin with.

"I am so sorry, Delia. I didn't even think about my shoulder or how I would hold you with one hand. Bad idea on my part."

"And silly of me to think it would work." She sighed. "No harm done."

"Except these bruises." He traced a hand down her cheek. "Too many bruises." She shivered under his soft, caring touch, and stepped back.

"Let's get this done. I need a hot bath and a drink."

"I can help with both of those."

"I am not getting into a tub with you around."

He held up his hands in mock surrender. "I have wine and a hot tub."

"Fine." She crossed her arms over her chest. "I accept."

Delia clipped the rope onto the boot and climbed back in. Nolan's arm was in a sling to take the pressure off his shoulder. She passed him the gifts, one by one, and he boxed them.

"There's a lot of great stuff here." She held up a stylish lady's jacket. "It's going to be a better Christmas for a lot of people."

When they were finished unloading and packing, the manager had two of his teenage staff carry the boxes out to the van. "Thanks, guys," Nolan said. He opened the passenger door and gestured for Delia to get in.

She climbed in, grunting with effort. She was going to hurt tomorrow. They turned the van and its contents over to the volunteers at the church and headed home.

Chapter Six

Nolan dropped his robe onto a chair and slid into the hot tub. He sat opposite Delia, who was leaning back, a plastic wineglass in her hand. No glass in, or near, the hot tub was one of his mother's cardinal rules.

"Oh, this feels great on my shoulder." He sighed in relief as blessed heat seeped in. He used the tub regularly, but tonight it was especially welcome. "How are you doing?" She'd been in the tub ten minutes already. He'd been distracted by a phone call from his folks and had urged her to go ahead.

"I'm good. I might ice my cheek later. One spot really aches." She touched her glass to her cheek.

The chilled wine must feel good against the swelling and growing bruise. "Did you want me to get you an ice pack? I don't mind." He didn't want to get out of the water and back into the freezing air, but if she needed ice, he'd get ice. Her grateful smile made the offer worthwhile.

"Thanks. I'm okay for now. I can ice it when I get home." She sipped her wine and leaned back with her eyes closed. "Today was fun. I didn't expect to enjoy myself. Of course, I didn't expect to get dropped on my head either." She gave him a one-eyed glare, though she didn't look all that angry.

"Accidents happen and someday, this will make a great story to tell your kids." Her glare doubled, so he added, "I can't apologize enough for dropping you. It was stupid macho thinking coupled with forgetting about my shoulder. I've probably set my healing back for months." He hoped not, but he couldn't undo what was done. "I enjoyed myself too."

"I came to town to escape the holiday excesses and parties. I thought that meant avoiding Christmas altogether. After today, I may have to rethink that strategy."

"It seems like so much effort to do anything special just for me."

"You could celebrate with friends."

"If I had any." He didn't mean to sound angry, but suspected he did.

"Come on now. You must have some friends. Everyone does."

"I broke contact with most of my fighting chums. Watching them was painful when I couldn't fight. I don't know many people in town. I guess I keep myself closed off. That adds up to no friends."

"You could reach out to your friends. Maybe not in time to share Christmas, but for later, in the new year. Maybe they'd have leads on jobs for you. I figure the more people in your court, the better. Half my city friends are keeping their ears open for me." She sighed. "But it's been a year, and I haven't found a job in advertising. I think my ex must have blacklisted me. It's tough to survive on a server's salary. It's a good thing I had savings from my contract."

"What contract is that?"

Her cheeks darkened.

"I wrote a book. It was a one-off."

"What does that mean?"

"I scratched it out a couple years ago and submitted it on a whim. They bought it. Sales were decent. Now, my publisher wants another one and I've got nothing." She slapped a hand on the water, sending droplets everywhere.

"What was the first about? Maybe we can brainstorm the second. Are they connected at all? I mean, is it a series, or are they stand-alone books?"

She explained the gist of the book without revealing the title or her pen name. I thought about taking the heroine and having her move to a new city and stumble upon another mystery.

"Wait! Are you talking about *Sunset Stalker*? By DL Regent? You're DL Regent? No way. I loved that book."

"Really? Thanks."

"You're going to have to autograph my copy. I borrowed it from the library and loved it enough that I got the hardback version. Where did the pen name come from?"

"My middle name is Regina. My boyfriend, who later became my fiancé, then my ex, didn't want people to know that I wrote dark books. It didn't fit his image. I went along with it because it didn't really matter to me. I morphed Regina to Regent. D for Delia. I just added the L because it worked for me."

"That's so cool. I feel privileged that you told me. I appreciate your trust in me."

"Ya, well, if the media finds out, I'll know who told them. Nobody knows but my brother and my publisher. And of course, my ex."

"Your secret is safe with me. Now, about that second book. I have a few ideas." They shared thoughts back and forth for a while.

"Oh, that's a good one. I can use that. Thanks. But I'll twist it and set it at Christmas. Make it a holiday classic, like *Iron Man 3*. I'm itching to write now. You've fired up my muse."

"*Iron Man 3 is* not a Christmas movie."

"Yes, it is." She sat up and set her glass down. "It takes place at Christmas, and several people have epiphanies about life." She clapped her hands together. "Boom. Christmas movie."

He laughed. "I don't know how many times I've had this argument. *Christmas Vacation* is a Christmas movie. *White Christmas* is too. There are hundreds, like *For the Love of Christmas*. Why try and pull in a movie that is clearly just an action thriller?" He shook his head. "With so many classics and new movies every year, I don't understand the reasoning."

"I used to love the holidays. I binge-watched holiday movies from October to February. Classics, new ones, romance. Anything Christmas." She sipped her wine. "Last year, when he dumped me, I went darker. I didn't want fluff and fun. I wanted more struggle and more sacrifice. *Iron Man 3* gave me that without being too dark. It's a fun movie, so I added it to my list. It reminded me that people can be redeemed, and that help comes from the strangest places."

He thought over her comments. Her breakup must have hit her hard. "I'm sorry you went through that."

"Thank you." After a moment, she said, "Look at us. Two sad sacks. Both of us lonely. Both our lives are dumpster fires. We both dislike the holidays. Both pitching in to help a charity do good work. I think I'll swing by the church tomorrow and see if Santa's Helpers need any assistance."

"Mind if I join you?" The offer came out of nowhere, but he realized with sudden clarity that he wanted to be there. He wanted to make a difference. He wanted to be part of the holidays.

Her brows knit together. "I don't see why not."

Chapter Seven

The church basement was a joyous disaster. People wearing Santa or elf hats rushed here and there. Tables practically groaned under the weight of donations. All around the edge of the enormous room, piles of unwrapped gifts stood waiting for the busy volunteers. Bright holiday music played in the background and the air was redolent with cocoa, coffee, and fresh baking.

Mrs. Anderson hurried up to them. "I'm so glad you came. We could use more hands."

"How can we help?" Delia asked, her attention firmly fixed on Mrs. Anderson.

"We've inventoried everything, but we're short quite a few gifts. It's always for the tweenagers. Nobody knows what to buy for them."

"It is a tough age," Delia agreed. "I remember just wanting money so I could buy my own gifts."

"We are in luck. Most of our families gave us lists of what their children want or need. But we need shoppers. Care to go shopping?" She gave them a hopeful look.

Delia glanced at Nolan, who looked anything but willing.

"I'd love to go," she lied. The last place she wanted to be was inside a store brimming with holiday goodness. She was warming up to the joy of the season, but wasn't ready for total inundation.

"I'll go with her. We came in my car."

"Excellent." Mrs. A. brushed her hands together in a 'that's done' gesture. "I'll get you our gift cards and the list. I can't thank you enough."

Ten minutes later, they stood in the hardware store. Delia glared at the boot as they passed. "I suppose we should check for gifts on our way out." The Santa hat Mrs. A. had insisted they wear slipped down over her eye. She straightened it with a sigh. Maybe Christmas wasn't bad, but having to wear this hat was over the top.

They made their way to the toy section and began selecting the items on the list. A young girl, three, maybe four years old, careened around the corner.

"Mandy Elizabeth Stone, you get back here right now." A harried woman carrying an infant and an enormous diaper bag raced after the girl.

"Whoa there." Nolan kneeled in the middle of the aisle. "Where are you going, little one?"

"Toys," she squealed. She looked up at Nolan, then at Delia. "Santa?" she whispered.

"Ho-ho-ho."

"Mama, look. Santa."

The woman frowned and took her daughter by the hand. "Come on dear, we just need a screwdriver. Then we can go."

"I wanna look at the toys! Santa, I want a new dolly."

"Come on, Mandy. The nice man doesn't have time for us today." A tear slipped down her cheek as she fumbled with clothing falling from the diaper bag.

"Santa always has time for little ones," Nolan said gently and sat on the dirty floor. "Come," he patted his knee. "Sit on Santa's lap and tell me what you want for Christmas."

Delia's heart melted. Her great, big, broad-shouldered neighbor was playing Santa for a child. She glanced at the woman. Her jacket was clean but tattered. She wore runners when boots would have been more appropriate. The baby's blanket had a couple of holes.

Holy broken angel wings.

Delia's heart filled with compassion. She glanced at Mandy as she climbed onto Nolan's lap with a shy smile. Her clothing was as worn as her mother's.

"Come on, Mandy. Don't bother the man. We have to go."

"Mama, it's Santa," Mandy pleaded. "Santa," she said earnestly. "I wants a doll, and a 'puter for Mama."

"A 'puter?" Nolan replied. "Tell me about that."

"A 'puter!" She looked at Nolan like he was dense. "So, Mama can do work. She solded hers to buy groceries when we moveded into the car."

Mandy's mother's face turned scarlet. "Let's go, Mandy. Say thank you to Santa."

"Thank you."

"Merry Christmas, Mandy."

The woman drug Mandy away without letting her look at the toys. "Santa might not come this year," she said in a heart-breaking tone.

"Oh, yes, he will," Delia vowed quietly.

"What do we do?" Nolan asked, rising to his feet.

They stared at each other for a moment. "I'm going to talk to her," Delia exclaimed.

"How do you even approach her?" He waved toward the end of the aisle where the small family had gone. "It's not easy to be in tough straits."

"Easy, we're Mr. and Mrs. Santa. We're going to give them a good Christmas."

They caught up with her two aisles over, looking at screwdrivers.

"Ma'am," Delia said cautiously. "Can I talk to you?"

"Yes?" Her voice trembled.

"I couldn't help but realize that you are in a tight spot. I'd like to help. We'd like to help." She waved to include Nolan.

"I'm not sure what you can do for me."

Delia hesitated. "Mandy said you live in your car. I'd like to offer you a temporary place to stay. I've got lots of room. A whole house. You can stay with me for a while. At least during this cold snap. Maybe we can help you find a job?"

"We'd love to help," Nolan put in. "Help you have a good Christmas."

"Thank you, but I don't think so. We're not staying in town."

"How about just one night? A warm bed and baths for the littles. And for you. A hot meal?" Delia pleaded, trying not to sound pushy. "No commitment after one night."

"Why?" The woman sniffed.

"Why? Because it's Christmas? Because you need a hand up? Because we can? I'm Delia. This is my neighbor, Nolan. Let us help you."

"I don't think so but thank you."

Delia pulled a paper and pen out of her pocket. "I can't force you to stay with me. But here's my address and phone number. If I'm not there, please wait. In a couple of hours, we'll be finished shopping for Santa's Helpers. I'd love to have you over, even if it is just to bathe the kids and have a hot meal." She pressed the paper into the woman's unresisting hand. "Think about it."

Three hours later, Delia slid a beef roast into the oven. There was a chocolate cake cooling on the counter, waiting to be iced.

"You know she's not coming, right." Nolan's voice was sad. "I wish she would."

"Me too, but if she does, I want to be prepared."

"I think the playpen Mom and Dad bought for my sister's kids is probably in the basement. I can go get it."

"Would you?" she asked excitedly.

"If she shows up, I will. I think I know where the sheets for it are too."

Impulsively she threw her arms around him in a grateful hug. "Thank you!'

The doorbell rang and she jerked back from him and raced to the front door. She flung it open.

The woman stood there, baby in her arms, Mandy at her side, a nervous look on her face. She shuffled her feet. "Hi." She looked down at the step.

"Come in out of the cold." Delia tugged her forward. "It's nice and warm in here. I just put a roast in the oven. Let me take your coat."

"Thank you. I'm sorry to intrude."

"No intrusion at all."

"Mama, look at the lights. The tree is bee-you-tee-full." She giggled and clapped her hands.

"Yes, it is."

"But there's no presents." Mandy's voice trembled.

"That's because it isn't Christmas yet," Nolan said from behind them.

"Santa!"

"Mandy," he said seriously, "My name is Nolan. I'm not Santa, I'm just Santa's special helper. It is very nice to meet you." He squatted down to her level and offered his hand.

Mandy looked at her mom.

"Shake Mr. Nolan's hand dear. Like this." She stepped forward and shook his hand. "I'm Aria. Nice to meet you, Nolan." Adorably, Mandy copied her mother.

"Come in. Take off your boots. Let me get your coat."

Nolan poured three mugs of decaf coffee and carried them to the table and grinned when Mandy's eyes widened at the plate of cookies Delia slid onto the table.

"Help yourself to a cookie."

"Just one," Aria warned her daughter as she buckled the baby, James, in the highchair Nolan had brought over from his house.

Mandy ate the cookie without leaving a single crumb. She guzzled her small glass of milk. "Thank you."

Nolan and Delia shared a soft smile.

"What changed your mind?" Delia asked.

"Honestly? Nothing would have made me swallow my pride and come here. Until my car died. It wouldn't start. I don't have enough money for repairs. I couldn't let my kids freeze. I begged a ride from an elderly lady." She sniffed. "I'm screwed. Totally screwed." She wept quietly for a moment.

Delia passed her a tissue.

"Mama?" Mandy's voice trembled.

"Mama will be fine," Nolan reassured her. "She just needs a minute. How about you and I go play in the other room?"

"There's a box of toys in the closet in the second bedroom," Delia said. "My brother's fiancée has two nieces."

"Let's wipe your fingers. We don't want to get crumbs all over the house." He quickly wiped Mandy's fingers and face and took her by the hand into the other room.

"It's so pretty," she exclaimed in awe.

"Yes, it is. Christmas can be beautiful." Mandy's joy swept into his heart, and for the first time in longer than he cared to admit, he had a heart filled with optimism and hope for the future. "Let's go find those toys."

Hand in hand, they climbed the stairs. Mandy nattered on about what she wanted for Christmas and about missing play school. Abruptly she proclaimed, "My dad gotted to go to heaven."

"Oh. You must be sad."

"Ya. But Mama says he's with the angels and that's a good place because now he's not sick no more."

"That's a very good thing." What else could he say? He wondered how long the man had been gone. How long had this small family been suffering? The baby seemed about eighteen months old, as far as he could tell. He hadn't thought to ask.

He made a mental note to let the organizers of the toy drive know about this family. If they didn't have enough to help them out, he'd find a way to do it himself.

"I'm so glad you came," Delia told Aria. "I'm really happy to have you here."

"I can't believe I'm here," Aria whispered. "My life is a total wreck."

"How can we help?"

"There's nothing you can do." Her tone was mournful. "I'm just destroyed since Davin died. I cry all the time. I can't afford childcare."

"Davin was your husband?"

"Yes. Cancer. Six months ago. Insurance didn't pay out. They repossessed our house. We've been living in the car."

"That's horrid. Aren't there any agencies that can help?"

"I don't even know where to start. It's so hard with the kids. We've been moving from town to town, trying to find a job."

"Well, your moving days are over," Delia declared. "You can stay here until you get a job, or until we find the right agency to help you get back on your feet."

"I can't ask you to do that." Tears streamed down her face.

"That's the beauty of it. You didn't ask. I'm offering. I called my brother earlier. This is his house. He said you're welcome to live here, with me. With him. His fiancée is happy to help too." She paused. "You only have one bag." She made the statement a question.

"What's left is in the car outside the grocery store. I've sold everything of value."

How tragic!

"We'll go over later and get your things and figure out what to do with your car. I'll pay to have it towed to the garage to see what's wrong. My brother's best friend owns the garage. He'll give it a once over for nothing." She'd spent her teen years avoiding her brother and his friend, who had teased her mercilessly. Jarrod owed her one. "I'll call him now."

Jarrod quickly agreed to tow the car for nothing and look at it in the morning. He'd swing by on his way home from work for the keys. He advised them to take anything of value out of the car before he got there.

"Why don't we get your things before dinner? We can clean the kids up and they'll be ready for bed right after we eat. You and Nolan can go. I'll watch the littles for you."

Aria hesitated. "I don't know..."

"You're nervous about leaving them with strangers. I get it. Why don't we send Nolan, then? He can bring back what you need."

She blushed beet red. "There isn't much." Her eyes glistened.

"Maybe not, but it's important to you. Why don't you give him the keys?"

Impossibly, she turned even redder. "I sold our suitcases."

Delia's heart broke for this poor woman. Then guilt flooded through her. She'd been complaining about her own hard times, which were nothing compared to what this woman was living. How selfish was she?

"I've got boxes he can use."

"Okay," she whispered and pulled the keys from her pocket.

Delia's heart wept for this poor broken woman and her adorable children.

Chapter Eight

"My mother always said Christmas is the time for miracles," Delia said as she scrambled eggs for breakfast. Aria stood alongside her, making toast while Mandy devoured a bowl of sugary cereal. The radio played softly in the corner and Elvis crooned about a white Christmas.

Aria smiled at Delia. "You are my miracle."

"Me? I'm just a regular person who saw someone who needed a hand, so I stuck mine out." She stirred the eggs. "I am more than happy to help."

"We appreciate it, and I'll find a way to repay you."

"Not me. Pay it forward. In years to come, help someone else out."

Nolan strode into the kitchen. "Morning, ladies." Over the past three days, he'd taken to coming and going at will. "I've got good news. I heard from my friend at the bank that the accountant's office is looking for a part-time receptionist."

Aria perked up and then looked sad. "I have no qualifications for a job like that."

"It says no experience necessary. They haven't posted it yet. I talked to their manager, and they'll wait to hear from you before they do."

"Why would he do that?" Aria frowned.

"Because I told him I had a friend who needed a job."

Tears ran down her face and she dashed them away. "Dang it. I'm always weeping." She started to smile, then frowned. "Dang it. I can't work part-time in an office. It won't pay enough to cover rent and childcare."

"The daycare is hiring. Maybe they'd let you bring your kids to work with you," Delia suggested. "I thought about applying, but it's so far out of my comfort zone that it terrifies me. You should apply for the job."

"But-"

"No buts," Nolan interrupted. "You've got nothing to lose and everything to gain."

Delia added, "Let's do up your resume after breakfast and you can walk it over. It's only a couple blocks."

Aria's face brightened. "You don't mind watching the kids while I do that?"

"Not at all. I enjoy them, and you won't be gone very long." Thankfully, Aria was beginning to trust them and see her and Nolan as friends.

After Aria departed, they settled Mandy down with a cartoon and sat in the kitchen with James in his high chair.

"What did the Santa's Helpers say?" she asked.

"They've got gifts for the kids, but they're running short on adult supplies."

"Darn it. I was hoping they'd have leftovers for Aria." She drummed her fingers on the side of her mug. "I'm going to dip into my savings and buy her a gift card for the clothing store. Everything she owns is in tatters."

"Her jacket looked nice," Nolan commented.

"That was one of my brother's fiancée's old ones. She had bagged it up to go to the charity. Unfortunately, there were no other clothes."

"The gift card is a good idea. I'll chip in too. Maybe she can get stuff for the kids as well." They enjoyed their coffee and plotted the best way to plan a wonderful Christmas for their new friends.

"You know what?" she asked.

"What?"

"I think I'm over hating Christmas." She grinned. "Seeing Aria struggle really knocked me out of my self-pity. I realize what a good life I have. And I have a good friend in you." She carried her mug to the sink. When she turned around, he was right beside her.

He cupped her chin in his hand. "Is that what this is?" he asked, a slight frown marring his brow. "Friends." He stared into her eyes. "I thought we were becoming more."

Her heart thumped. *Holy crap on a cracker. Were they a thing? Did she want them to be a thing?* Her mind whirled and her chest tightened.

"Are we?" she whispered.

"I think we are." His breath whispered over her lips.

Lord above, she was falling for this big-hearted man. This could be heaven, or it could be a disaster. Neither of them were in a stable job. Or had a job at all. She had a wounded heart. He had a wounded body. Suddenly, she didn't care.

"If you don't stop me," he whispered, "I'm going to kiss you."

She licked her lips. "Okay," the single word whispered out with a sigh of anticipation.

He studied her for a moment longer, and she wondered what he was looking for. He swooped in and brushed his lips across hers and, abruptly, she forgot to think at all.

Lightning raced over her body. Her pulse pounded in her ears. Kissing Nolan was bliss. Not just because he was an amazing kisser, but because being in his arms felt like being home. Excitement, arousal, and bliss swooped together, and her knees went weak. Sweat heaven.

"Are you gonna marry Dee?" Mandy asked.

They jerked apart.

Delia caught Nolan's eye, and they started to laugh.

"I really like Delia," Nolan answered. "But we're not ready to get married yet."

Disappointment flooded her heart, though the words were true. They barely knew each other.

"Mama says people kiss when they are getting married."

"Does she?" Delia asked.

The little girl nodded sagely. "And Christmas is for love and miracles." She smiled like she had a secret. "Kissing is love."

"I'm not sure we're in love yet," Delia said. "But I like Nolan a lot."

"You should kiss him again and find out. Mama says sometimes you have to try things more than once to know if you like them. Like broccle-trees." She stuck out her tongue. "I hate it. It's gross." She turned and left the kitchen.

They stared after her, and as one, started to chuckle.

"Kids say the darndest things," Nolan quipped. He pivoted her face back to face him. "I think we should test her theory." He lifted one brow.

"I think you're on to something."

Nolan couldn't stop thinking about their sweet kisses. He should be focused on the drive downtown to pick up gift cards for Aria. Instead, he kept reminiscing and sneaking glances at Delia. Something about the woman beside him had him captivated. She'd gone from surly to cheerful. From disliking Christmas to being all in on giving Aria the best Christmas possible. She had even volunteered to babysit while Aria did her first training shifts at the daycare this week. She'd start full-time the first Monday after Christmas.

Delia was starting her new job as a receptionist on the same day. That left him as the only unemployed one in their group. He wasn't physically strong enough yet to do manual labor and wasn't qualified for much else.

He toyed with the idea of asking his parents to lend him startup capital to open a martial arts studio, but the prideful coward in him wouldn't admit that he might need help.

"You're thinking very hard," Delia said. "Your face is all scrunched up. What's bothering you? It's only days until Christmas. You should be happy."

"Just thinking. Nothing to worry yourself over." He grimaced. "Sorry, I didn't mean for that to sound so condescending. I've got a lot on my mind lately."

"You're thinking about the future, aren't you?"

How had she guessed?

"A bit."

Her laugh startled him. "More than a bit. Over the past few days, you've become more and more preoccupied."

No, he'd returned to the preoccupation he'd had before she exploded into his life with her basket of muffins.

"I've been out of the game for nearly eight months. That's a long time. I don't know where to go with my life."

"You should open a place of your own. Teach some beginner classes to start. Maybe hire a few people to teach the things you can't yet do."

It was startling that her suggestion mirrored his thoughts.

"I can't afford that. I have almost no savings left. That means no startup capital. It takes money to run a business."

"What about a partner? Or a loan? Or see if your family wants to invest in you?"

"I won't ask my parents for money. They've supported me for too long already. A man has his pride."

Her stare made him uncomfortable.

"Don't you think they'd want you to succeed? To move on with your life? I'd like to think that if my parents were still alive, they'd give me a helping hand."

"I don't want to talk about it." He parked in front of the hardware store. He'd been in this lot more in December than he had been his entire time in Crackleberry Ridge. "Let's just hit the clothing store for that gift card."

"And the drugstore as well."

"I can't believe that you're all-in to give Aria a hand up, but you won't take one yourself."

"Drop it."

"Well then, ask your banker friend for a small business loan."

"On what collateral?"

"How about this hundred-thousand-dollar car? Do you have a loan on it? Couldn't it be collateral?"

"Drop it." He jumped out of the car and glared at her over the hood. "Let's just finish this. I have things to do at home."

"Bah humbug."

Barely speaking to each other, they got gift cards for Greta's Glad Rags, Filman's Drugs, Boxer's Shoes, and The Tasty Pastry Bakery. Most of the money was for clothing as it seemed to be Aria's biggest need aside from baby staples which Santa's Helpers had been happy to provide.

As they headed home, she said, "I think you should reconsider your stubborn, independent stance. People are willing to help others. You never know until you ask. What was it you told Aria? You don't know unless you ask."

"How many times do I have to tell you to drop it?" He glared. "Let it go. Mind your own business."

No one said another word as they drove the short distance to their duplexes. Each of them was so lost in their own angry thoughts that the tension between them was like a third person in the car.

And to think he believed he was falling for her. She was just a nosy busybody. He'd been right to think her a giant pain the night she arrived. He couldn't wait to get home and out of this car.

Chapter Nine

DECEMBER 19TH

I t was well past nine when Mandy finally fell asleep. As Christmas grew closer, she became increasingly excited. She was young but had caught on to the concept of Santa bringing presents on Christmas morning. Delia had taken her to the store for special pajamas for Christmas Eve. While they were there, she pretended not to notice Nolan buying socks.

It had been three days since he shut her out. She'd called and texted every day trying to apologize for stepping into his business. He didn't answer the calls or respond to the texts. She knew he heard the calls because she could hear his phone ringing through their adjoining wall.

"That child is going to wear me right out." Aria dropped into a chair with a heavy sigh. "I really can't thank you enough for all that you've done. You've watched my kids, helped me find a job, made Christmas possible, and given me a home. I owe you so much."

"This isn't a one-way street. You've given me back the joy of Christmas through your family."

"Funny. You don't seem that happy. You've been moping for days."

"I have not."

"Look, we may not have been friends for long, but I won't lie to a friend. You turned grumpy the day Nolan stopped coming around. What happened? I thought you were a thing."

"I barely know the man." She huddled into the corner of her brother's huge navy couch and pulled a pillow onto her lap.

"Really? Mandy said you guys were kissing. You've been together every day and get along well. That doesn't seem like barely knowing him."

"I met him December first when I arrived in town. I came to watch my brother's house."

"Did you leave a job to be here?" She looked sympathetic. "We really haven't talked much about you."

"I was dumped and fired by my ex at Christmas time last year. I came here to escape him and the holidays. Ironic right?" She waved at all the holiday paraphernalia around the living room. "Nolan thought I had broken in and sent the police to arrest me."

Aria laughed. "That's a hilarious meet-cute."

"This is not a romance novel." Her new friend was obsessed with contemporary romance and read several library books a week. Delia had given them up when she was dumped. She'd probably never read another one, though the progress on the mystery she was writing was astoundingly good. "This is real life." She dropped her head to her chest and huffed out a frustrated breath. "He's a good guy. But he's stubborn and doesn't listen to reason."

"He *is* a decent man. Look at everything he's helped you do for us." She was silent for a moment. "Maybe he needs time to adjust. Losing your career, especially when it is your passion, can be a huge blow."

"True." She hated that Aria was right. "He's just so stubborn."

"He's a man!"

Delia's laugh was wry. "Truth." She was silent for a few minutes and contradictory thoughts rolled through her head, battering her heart with a whip of tangled emotions. "I just don't get why he won't ask for help."

"Did you?"

"No." She wrinkled her nose and shook her head. "I managed."

"Look, he's a guy. Men are stubborn. Loveable but stupidly stubborn. I know that in his position, my husband would have resisted asking for help. He worked two jobs while I was pregnant, just so I could stay off my feet. James was a difficult pregnancy for me. Men want to, no, they need to be providers. It's in their genes. Just like the majority of women are nurturers. Sure, there are exceptions. What rule doesn't have them? Just cut him some slack. Give him time to realize that maybe your ideas weren't all bad."

"You know that it's part of the girl code to always take your girlfriend's side. You know that, right?"

"Conventionally, yes. But in this case. It's my duty, via the code, to tell you when you are wrong. A good friend sets her friend straight."

"Fine." She mock pouted. Aria was right. Maybe she'd pushed too hard. Maybe she should let him be for a while.

Or maybe not.

"You know what? I let my jerk-face ex push me around. I'm no-body's pushover. I'm going to stand up for myself and for Nolan."

"Indeed?"

"Only I don't know what to do. How do I help?"

"Setting aside the fact that he obviously doesn't want help. If this were a romance novel..."

Delia rolled her eyes.

"This is a time for the grand gesture."

"Doesn't the guy do that?"

"Usually. But I'm all about women standing up for themselves. Why shouldn't the grand gesture be yours? Prove yourself to him."

"It's only been three weeks since we met. We've gone out exactly three times. Most of our time together was with Santa's Helpers."

"Oh, Delia. The heart wants what the heart wants. Love doesn't know any timelines."

"I don't love him," she protested. "I just like him. A lot."

"Let me put it this way. Are you willing to risk losing him by doing nothing? Are you willing to put yourself out there for a chance at a future with him?"

"What if it doesn't go anywhere? What if we crash and burn?"

"You already have. Now, be like the phoenix. Rise from the ashes of your mistakes and fly free. Soar with your heart. Love doesn't have any guarantees. Trust me on this. I know."

"But you loved and lost." She couldn't fathom the pain Aria had gone through. How did you even survive losing your heart's love?

"And I'd do it all again, even knowing it would end too soon. Our love was worth it. Even if we hadn't had children, it was worth every second of the pain and sorrow." She looked pleadingly at Delia. "Think about it."

"Thank you for seeing me." Delia twisted her hands together and wiggled on the padded bank chair in the manager's office. Jeff Isaacs was an imposing man. Tall and broad-shouldered, he looked like he could bench press a Smart Car. He was nothing like she expected.

"What can I do for you, Miss Becker? It is Miss?"

"Miss. Ms. I don't have a preference. But please, call me Delia." She wiped her palms on her slacks surreptitiously.

"Okay then, Delia. What can I do for you? Are you looking for a loan? For what purpose?" He folded his hands together on the desk and leaned forward like he couldn't wait to hear what she had to say.

"Not exactly. No." She swallowed hard. "I'm not here for me."

He frowned. "I can't lend you money for someone else." He sat back, no longer interested.

"Wait. Let me explain."

"It's about Nolan Tayler," she blurted.

"What about him?"

"He said you know him. He'll kill me if he knows I came here." She twisted her hands together again and then took a large swallow from her water bottle.

"Is there a point? I don't discuss other people's business. It's unprofessional." He fidgeted with a gold pen on his pristine desk blotter.

"Okay. Can you just hear me out? No need for you to say anything. Just listen. Please." He nodded, so she mustered her courage and started talking.

"You know Nolan was due to make it big in the MMA world. You know he got hurt and can never fight competitively again. What he can do is teach. I've seen him working out. He's amazing. Those Karate dance things he does...what are they called?"

"Katas."

"His katas are incredible. He's great with kids. He's a very generous and giving man." The banker's eyebrow lifted. "Never mind all that. I think he would open a martial arts studio and teach the disciplines he excels at if he had the money."

Jeff said nothing.

"All I'm asking is that you consider giving him a loan. Or find a way to help him out. He says he has no friends, but he knows people all over town. He's been giving our roommate, Aria, a helping hand." She quickly related Aria's story. "I think he needs a helping hand, too. To get back on his feet. Just consider it. Okay?"

"Miss Becker, Delia. I won't discuss my friends, their finances, loans, or businesses with anyone except them. Same goes for customers. But I do thank you for this information."

He stood. Clearly, the interview was over.

She sighed. She'd hoped for more. "Thank you for seeing me." At the door, she paused and turned back toward him. "Think about it." Shelving her disappointment, she headed home.

Nolan strode into the coffee shop and scanned the customers. Jeff Isaacs, one of his thug friends from high school, waved him over. He

grabbed a coffee and muffin and wove his way to the back. Jeff stood to greet him with a man-hug, complete with back-slapping.

"How are you doing?" Jeff asked, sliding back onto the vinyl bench.

"I'm great. I see you're still rocking the banking world. Nice suit, by the way."

"Thanks. There was a day I never thought I'd be respectable. Your troubles helped me see the light. I straightened up before I got arrested. I did grade twelve twice."

"I didn't know that. I thought you shot right off to college."

"Confession time. I went to Camrose and repeated a year. Then I went to college."

"That's awesome, man." Nolan flipped the lid off his reusable take-out cup and sipped. Double cream, just the way he liked it, and cool enough to drink almost instantly. "I was surprised to hear from you."

They'd chatted now and then when they bumped into each other, but never really struck up a friendship. Their worlds were just too far apart.

"I heard a rumor that you need money."

Nolan pushed back his chair, nearly upsetting it, and jerked to his feet. "This conversation is over."

"Sit down. Hear me out."

Nolan glared for a full minute before sitting. *Who the hell had told Jeff about his troubles? Someone was in trouble.* "Who told you?"

"That doesn't matter." He made a shooing motion as if pushing that part of their conversation aside. "Let's say a little bird told me you were thinking about opening a dojo, or martial arts studio."

"Considering. Not doing."

"I'm going out on a limb and saying that funding is an issue."

Nolan bit back a snarky response.

"Look, man. I watched you fight. I was your biggest fan. In fact, I went to three fights in Vegas just to see you win. You have skills. You might not be able to fight, but I think you could teach."

"What gave you that idea?" He was so done with this conversation.

"That little bird told me about your work in Santa's Helpers, and what you've done for that needy family. That makes you my type of people, and a good risk."

"Good risk, bad risk. I can't afford to open a studio."

"Maybe not, but I can."

"I beg your pardon." He wasn't hearing what he thought he heard. No way.

"I make good money. I've made a lot of great investments. This town needs a new martial arts place. I don't care what discipline. The teens need a place to learn to work off frustrations. I need a place to spar. You run the place, I'll put up the money, and a couple of guys I know could teach part-time. I think we could make a go of it. Your name will draw in fighters from across the country. Granted, you're no Forrest Griffin or Sean O'Malley. But you have a solid reputation. You're a clean fighter with an impressive record. This could work."

The hope that had vanished after his disagreement with Delia threatened to blossom again. "Why me?" he asked half belligerently.

"Because you're the best man for the job. Because I like to invest. Because my six-year-old son is turning into an asshole like we were. I think you can help."

"That's one hell of a burden to put on someone."

"Hey, you win, I win. You don't straighten him out, no blame, no foul."

"This is all rather sudden." His mind boiled with thoughts. Ideas for the school. Where he'd build it. Who he'd hire. How he'd make it work. He'd dreamed of this. But he was waiting for the other shoe to drop. There had to be a catch.

"Who told you about this?" He had a hunch. Not even his parents knew of this dream. He'd kept it secret from almost everyone.

"I'm not at liberty to say."

He cussed. "Delia."

The shock on Jeff's face told him he'd hit home.

"I'll throttle her. This was none of her business." He stood. "I think we're done here." He stormed out of the café and kicked a pine cone off the sidewalk. "Stupid trees."

He was halfway home when he remembered that he'd driven to meet Jeff.

"Crap on toast."

"Pardon me?" A blue-haired old lady gave him a stern look.

"Pardon me, ma'am."

She stopped short. "As I live and breathe. Nolan Tayler. Son of a gun." She thrust out her hand. "Honored to meet you. Sorry about your accident."

"Um. Thanks?" He raised one eyebrow in question. Who was this?

"Marion Hughes. You fought my grandson. Dirty Dog Hughes. You kicked his ass. Showed that whipper snapper a thing or two. Good, that you knocked him down a peg. He's a better man now."

He remembered Dirty Dog. He was a mean fighter and cheated at every opportunity. As he fumbled for something nice to say, she continued.

"You teaching somewhere? I want a class."

She wanted to learn to fight? She had to be seventy.

"Do they do senior's self-defense? A girl's gotta protect herself. Pumping iron ain't enough." She flexed her arm, though it made no difference under her bulky coat.

"No plans to teach, ma'am."

"Stop with that, ma'am stuff. It's Marion. You start teaching. I need the workout. See you around." She walked away; her steps faster than he could have imagined for someone her age. Watching her go, he felt like he was a hundred and two.

"Why does it feel like the universe is trying to tell me something?"

Chapter Ten

DECEMBER 24TH

It was barely past five and Delia had been awake for hours, pounding away on her laptop. In a record burst of anger infused inspiration, she had pounded out six chapters of her next book. Now, silence reigned in her house, and behind the wall she shared with Nolan. Was he awake and restless, too?

"Why can't I stop thinking about him?" She stared out the kitchen window into the darkness. Their friendship had known a few ups and downs. In hindsight, it was funny that he'd sicced the cops on her. And she couldn't blame him for being upset at her for her early morning muffin drop. "Think before you act. Why didn't I remember that?"

Last night, inspiration had hit. The first time she'd annoyed him, she'd made and taken him muffins. He said he liked them. He was upset with her again. Maybe something hot and tasty would help.

She hadn't made monkey buns for years. Not since college. But she knew the recipe by heart and, as luck would have it, her brother had frozen raw dinner rolls in the freezer. A trick they'd learned from their mother who had always kept them on hand.

She'd prepped the simple mock cinnamon buns last night and now they were cooling on the counter.

Finally, a light flashed outside. She peered out the window. "Yes!" Nolan's kitchen light glowed in his backyard. "Here we go." She slid her hands into a pair of Christmas oven mitts and picked up the buns.

"All right universe, I'm giving it my best shot with apology buns. Probably can't make it worse," she muttered. "He's already not talking to me. Nothing ventured, nothing gained."

They'd probably never get back to the place where they shared a kiss, but maybe they could be friends. Or at least friendly neighbors. He'd probably move on to a new town and she'd stay here. She loved her job at the accounting firm. A surprising variety of people came in and out in a steady stream. Whatever happened with Nolan, she wanted it to be positive. Positive from now on, or a positive ending.

She pounded on his door with the toe of her slipper. Hopefully, he heard the muffled thumps. She should have worn boots. She waited. And waited. And waited.

He wasn't coming.

Dejected, she headed back down the sidewalk.

"Do I have to call the cops on you again?" he called out.

She whirled round, nearly losing her grip on the hot pan. She opened her mouth to snap back at him. He was grinning.

She edged back to the base of the steps and looked up at him. Glory be. He looked amazing, all sleep-mussed and tousled. "Pretty sure we don't need to bring the law into this."

"That depends?" His eyes sparkled.

"Depends on what?" She squinted at him. Something was up, but she couldn't figure out what.

"Depends on what's in that pan."

"That's for me to know and for you to find out. Can I come in?" Snow drifted down around her. Christmas Eve snow had been a favorite when she was a kid. It always brought good luck.

He tapped his lips with his finger. "I suppose." He drew the word thoughtfully.

"Thank you for your gracious invitation." She picked her way carefully up the snowy steps and slipped past him. Without further invitation, she kicked off her slippers, went into the kitchen, and set the pan on the stove. "Is there coffee?"

"Always." Something in his tone made her turn to face him.

"It's cinnamon buns," she blurted, discomfited by his strange behavior. He didn't seem mad anymore, but she couldn't put her finger on what his mood was. He kept smirking. Was he laughing at her?

"Really? I love cinnamon buns. Do you have any idea how hard it was to resist them when I was training? I would have killed for one." In a flash, he was right beside her, fork in hand. "These smell amazing." He stabbed one roll, yanked it out, and took a bite.

He fanned his mouth and mumbled. "Shoot. Hot." He chewed and swallowed. "Pecans? Sweet mercy on a motorbike."

"What?"

He held up a finger in a wait gesture. He chowed down the bun in record time. While she waited, she found mugs and poured them coffee. She set two rolls on plates on the table and sat.

"Thank you," he said, his voice warm with gratitude.

"It's just a mock cinnamon bun." She shook her head. Maybe he'd gotten into a fight and had his marbles knocked loose.

"Not for that. For talking to Jeff."

She blinked, not sure what to say.

"He called me." He slid into the chair across from her.

"And?"

"We're going into business together. He's my silent partner. He'll put up the funds, I'll provide the labor. We'll split the profits. You were right. I needed the nudge. This has been a dream for years. I was just afraid to take a chance. Or to ask for help."

"I'm happy for you." She was, but she was still feeling odd about his attitude.

"Seriously. I owe my future to you. The day I tried to have you arrested was the best day of my life." He reached across the table and grabbed her hands. "I was so angry when Jeff told me someone had approached him on my behalf. I fumed for days. Then reality hit. I was resisting for no reason beyond my pride."

She kept silent, sensing he wasn't finished.

"Then I thought about Mandy and Aria. Aria bit down her pride and took our help. If she could do it, so could it. I called Jeff back, and we worked out some details. There's a lot to figure out and so much planning to do. But I'm doing this and it's all thanks to you. Thank you, Delia. Thank you so much." He squeezed her hands.

"You're welcome."

"There's just one thing."

"What's that?"

He jumped to his feet and pulled her to hers. "Just this." He paused and stared into her eyes. "I hope I haven't chased you away." Slowly, giving her plenty of time to resist, he came closer until she felt his breath on her lips.

"To heck with this." She pushed upward, crashing her mouth into his. "You're forgiven," she mumbled against his lips.

The kiss lasted only seconds but felt like a beautiful eternity. She committed every second to her memory. When they came up for air, she whispered, "Merry Christmas, Nolan."

He picked her up and swung her around. "Merry Christmas, Delia."

Epilogue

One Year Later

"Hurry up, Nolan. We're going to be late."

"Aria and Mandy will wait, and James has no idea what Christmas is," he called from upstairs. His parents had retired to the west coast and after Halloween, she'd moved in with Nolan.

"Mandy won't wait. She's a kid. Kids want to open their gifts immediately. They don't want to wait for slothful old men."

He jogged down the stairs carrying an enormous gift bag and wearing a huge grin. "I am not a slothful old man. I'm a fit MMA instructor and coach."

"Sloth."

"Early bird." He pecked her on the lips. "Let's go."

They hurried next door. Kyle had moved in with Cindy and was renting his house to Aria for a very reasonable price. They let themselves into Christmas chaos.

"About time you got here," Kyle called out.

Mandy careened around the corner. "Yay. Now we can open the presents. Santa came!" She didn't stop. She raced into the living room and slid to a stop under the tree.

Opening the gifts was pure, blissful chaos. Delia loved every second of it. When the mess was cleaned up, she snuggled into Nolan's side on the couch.

"Thanks for the books," he said. "I can't wait to read them." She'd given him a selection of books on the history of martial arts. He probably knew a lot already, but like her, he'd become an avid reader. They spent hours together cuddled up with their books and with each other.

"Thanks for the snow globe. It's perfect." She had no idea where he'd found one with a police car in front of a tiny house with a uniformed officer on the step.

"Oh. I got you something else." He stood and dug into his pocket. Her heart hitched.

He dropped to one knee. "Delia, you arrested my heart the first time I saw you." Someone groaned at the pun and he shot them a finger behind his back. Delia laughed. "We've had our fights. This last year has been the best year of my life. You gave me back my joy in life. You gave me hope, a career. I just need one more thing from you."

She waited, her hands trembling in her lap.

"Will you do me the honor of becoming my wife?" He held out a simple engagement ring of tiny diamonds and emeralds.

"Yes!" She threw herself into his arms, knocking him over. Luckily, the coffee table was in the basement to make room for the morning's messy fun. "Yes. Yes. Yes." She punctuated her words with kisses.

"Thank heaven," he muttered. "I was so freaked that you'd say no."

"I told you that kissing meant married," Mandy said, hands on her hips. "I warned you." She sounded exactly like her mother. Everyone laughed.

"Merry Christmas, Nolan."

"Merry Christmas, Delia."

Author's Note

If you've been reading my books for a while, you've probably noticed that I adore Christmas. The gifts, the decorations, the food. Mostly, I love that we all take the time to be kinder to others and to offer a helping hand.

This story came from a helping hand. My dear friend Rexx told me a sweet and funny story about the time he was collecting gifts for charity and dropped his daughter into Santa's boot. Luckily, she was unharmed. He suggested that it would make a great story.

I hope you found it as amusing as I did.

Thanks for reading.

Katie

About Katie

Alberta romance author Katie O'Connor can't live without her computer and eReader, and her favorite place to use them is in the woods while watching the deer frolic on her summer property, Sanctuary. Her passion, aside from romance and her grandbabies, is giving back to the writing community. She's always eager to share what she's learned about writing and romance. In 2025, she will be a Story Coach in the Alexandra Writers' Center's Author Development Program. She's fueled by coffee and steak, and is fluent in sarcasm, cussing, dad jokes, and romantic jargon. If you need her, she'll be cozied up by the coffee pot eyeing the cookies.

Where to Find Katie

Website: https://katieohwrites.com

Email: katie@katieohwrites.com

Mailchimp Signup: http://eepurl.com/Q2nRr

Facebook: http://www.facebook.com/katieohwrites

Bookbub: https://www.bookbub.com/profile/katie-o-connor

Instagram: https://www.instagram.com/katieohwrites/

Goodreads: https://www.goodreads.com/author/show/5362469.
Katie_O_Connor

Katie O'Connor's Books

A Silver Fox Christmas:
Their Christmas Heart
Their Christmas Love
Their Perfect Christmas
A Silver Fox Christmas Box Set

Hearts Haven:
Running Home
Building Trust
Saving Grace
Heart's Haven Box Set

Three Moon Falls:
Fire Magic
Water Magic
Earth Magic

Stand Alone Books:
Carly's Heart
Matchmaker Christmas
Cupid's Charm
Gingerbread Dreams
Christmas in Silver Creek
Fake Dating at Half Moon Bay
Playing for Keeps in Half Moon Bay
Sleigh Bells Inn
Hearts in the Spotlight
To a Tea
Bulletproof Heart

Protecting Josie
Rekindled Fire
Winning Her Love
Ticket to Her Heart

Coming Soon:
Air Magic

www.ingramcontent.com/pod-product-compliance
Lightning Source LLC
Chambersburg PA
CBHW051310170626
46809CB00004B/1836